MARCO SOLO

written by

James Schwinn and Gail Harlow

illustrated by Andrew Turner

Reverse Angle

Reverse Angle Productions Incorporated
Philadelphia

Published 1995 by Reverse Angle Productions Incorporated
2 Penn Center Plaza
Philadelphia, Pennsylvania 19102

813
S415m

Layout and jacket design by Greg Concha

Printed in the United States of America

10 9 8 7 6 5 4 3 2 1

A Marco Solo Story

Publisher's Cataloging-in-Publication Data

Schwinn, James.
Marco Solo / written by James Schwinn and Gail Harlow ;
illustrated by Andrew Turner.
p. cm.
LCCN: 95-071832.
ISBN 0-9649006-0-2

Summary: A curious young boy from the inner city boards a local commuter train, looking for relief from the summer heat, and finds more than just shade on his journey.

I. Harlow, Gail. II. Turner, Andrew, ill. III. Title.

PZ7.S349Mar 1995   [Fic]

The art for each illustration consists of an acrylic on canvas painting.

Special thanks to The Sande Webster Gallery, Philadelphia.

Reinforced Binding & Running Glossary

For Anthony

Dear Reader,

We live close to the tracks. So when I lie awake in my bed late at night, long after my mother has turned out the light, I sometimes hear the sound of trains rumbling by. I wonder where they're going, where they've been. Then I wonder where I'm going, where I've been.

I wonder mostly because there's so much I don't understand, like why my father left me and my mother three years ago, and why some of the houses on our street are boarded up so people can't live in them anymore...and why kids 'round here sometimes get shot.

I wonder about these things for a while, then maybe think about tomorrow's baseball game or my homework assignment—stuff I can do something about. What do you think about when you lie awake in your bed late at night?

Some days, like the one in the story you're about to read, I just want to get away from the jumble and noise of my neighborhood and explore a place I've never been. Lots of kids around here never leave the 'hood. Others leave and never come back. I like visiting strange new places, seeing how other people live. But I always come back. Maybe someday my father will come back, too.

Marco Jennings stood on the platform, his baggy jeans and T-shirt flapping in *rhythm* with the wind as he waited for the next train. Across the platform, he saw grown-ups, some of them black, some of them white, most of them a color in between. They wore dark suits and carried heavy briefcases. "Corp'RAT America," his father used to call these people. "They make lots of money." For a moment or two, Marco stared at the *corp'RATs* across the tracks. Then he looked down and scraped his sneakers

Rhythm: Rappers use it, jazz has it. It may not always rhyme...but it's gotta have a beat...like Marco in the breeze...away from city heat

Across the platform, he saw grown-ups, some of them black, some of them white, most of them a color in between. They wore dark suits and carried heavy briefcases.

Corp'RATs: Businesspeople caught in the "rat race," easily identified by their dark suits, heavy briefcases and cellular phones.

against the platform's edge, *his* platform's edge.

He wasn't sure why he'd headed to the train station this morning. School was out for the summer. The community pool was closed for repairs, and the long, hot July days seemed to run together like melting taffy. One thing Marco knew—he'd rather be someplace where the pavement felt cool under his feet.

Marco still missed his father—particularly when he
saw other kids in the neighborhood going places with
their dads.

Marco wondered if that was how his father felt the day he left. The image of his father walking away—his scuffed basketball tucked under one arm, a battered suitcase under the other—flashed into his mind as he stared across the tracks. The first few months his father was gone, his mother kept saying, "He'll be back. He's just gotta get basketball out of his system." Well, three years had gone by now, and his mother didn't say that so much anymore.

Marco had stopped looking for his father's name on game rosters long ago. But he still missed his father—particularly when he saw other kids in the neighborhood going places with their dads. Seeing them pal around like that reminded him of the times his father had shown him fancy moves on the *makeshift* court in the alley behind their rowhouse. Marco hadn't picked up a basketball since the day his father left.

Baseball was his game now. He was a pitcher and threw a wicked curve—so wicked, in fact, the kids on his team called him "Snapper." Snapper Jennings. Marco liked his nickname. It sounded good. "Good enough to pitch big league someday," he liked to hear himself say. *"Yeah...maybe,"* a smart-aleck voice inside his head always answered back.

Makeshift: Not the real thing, but it'll do.

As a train approached corp'RAT America's platform, Marco *fiddled* with the loose change in his pocket and tried to imagine what it would be like to be one of those corp'RATs, racing down their side of the tracks every day. For an instant, he saw himself *sandwiched* in a sea of suits, being carried onto the train by a *riptide* of blue pinstripe.

"Next stop, Newark!" he heard the conductor bellow after all the suits had boarded. Slowly, the 7:01 pulled out of the station. Marco peered down the tracks. In the distance, he saw a light flicker. His train was approaching.

Climbing aboard, Marco took a seat next to the window and looked out as his neighborhood passed by: red, pink and blue rowhouses...the community garden...Donovan's Bar...*ramshackle* warehouse shells, swimming in weeds behind barbed-wire fences...picked-over skeletons of abandoned cars...broken brown bottles...scrunched-up bags from Mickey-D's.

A few minutes later, the conductor came to collect Marco's fare. Marco pulled an assortment of change out of his pocket and handed it over. "How far can I go?" he asked the conductor in a cocky voice, wanting to ride as far as the tracks would take him. "Allen's Lane is as far as you can get on this if you want to make it back home," the conductor answered gruffly, after he'd counted up the money. His *"I'm not gonna take any nonsense from you"* glare reminded Marco of Mr. Shackleford, his teacher in school, who was always telling him that no matter how smart he thought he was he could do better. The conductor handed him back a quarter and his return ticket. Marco *hunkered down* and stared at the vinyl back of the seat in front of him. Before he knew it, the conductor was calling out, "Al-LEN'S Lane!"

Fiddle: To play with something...like a coin or bottle cap, or maybe even a violin.
Sandwiched: Caught in the middle, like ham and cheese between two slices of rye.
Riptide: A very strong force, like a current of water, that will carry you away if you don't watch out.

"How far can I go?" he asked the conductor in a cocky voice, wanting to ride as far as the tracks would take him.

Ramshackle: Almost ready to collapse—don't sneeze!
Hunker down: To crouch, squat, scrunch yourself into place for a long stay.

Four women in brightly colored running suits huffed by. "We□
His mother was too busy to jog, working all day as a nurse's aide□

arco got off the train and began to walk. The houses were bigger here. There was grass in front of them and behind. An old man carrying a clear plastic bag walked his dog on a leash along the sidewalk. Four women in brightly colored running suits huffed by. Heads up! Eyes straight ahead! One of them even wore makeup. Marco chuckled a little as he glanced their way. Were *these* corp'RAT wives?

His mother seldom wore lipstick or mascara, and she was too busy to jog, working all day as a nurse's aide at the hospital 12 blocks from their home. Before his father left, she had been studying to become a nurse—a real nurse. Now she often had to work two shifts to pay the bills, and there was no time for school. Marco knew she still dreamed about becoming a nurse someday. He wished there was something he could do to help her.

Exploring the neighborhood, Marco walked down a long, winding street, past houses as large as his school and larger than the Church of the Reliable Redeemer he went to most Sundays with his mother. A mild breeze blew, cooling the air and spreading sweet smells of budding roses and freshly cut grass. As he walked, he felt his body begin to relax. "This is going to be an all right day," he thought.

hese corp'RAT wives?" Marco wondered.
he hospital 12 blocks from their home.

Marco picked up the ball. It felt good in his hands.

Ricochet: Bounce off this, boomerang off that. Zip, zap, zing! Better keep your head down.

Passing a green-shuttered house, Marco noticed a boy about his age dribbling a ball in the driveway and throwing it toward a hoop attached to the wall of a large garage. He threw and missed, and threw again and missed again. The ball *ricocheted* off the rim each time with a loud twang.

After the second throw, the ball bounced down the driveway and came to rest on the sidewalk in front of Marco. Marco picked up the ball. It felt good in his hands. He looked at the boy. The boy looked back suspiciously. Marco fingered the ball, unsure at first what to do. The boy said nothing. Then Marco dribbled the ball a couple of times and tossed it back. The boy made an awkward-looking catch. "Thanks," he said, in a low, mumbly voice, staring *intently* at Marco. "No problem," said Marco.

"Hey, Chris!" he heard someone shout as two boys made a break for the driveway from the porch in front of the house. "Pass me the ball," one of them said, then proceeded to sink a basket with a satisfying swoosh. *"Aw-right, Nick!"* Chris exclaimed. Marco looked on for a second, then turned away, figuring he wasn't going to be asked to play...not knowing what he'd say if he were.

"Who's that? What's he doin' here?" Marco heard the one called Nick ask as he walked away. "Dunno...haven't seen him around before," Chris replied, tossing the ball against the garage door. The three boys paused to watch Marco leave, then went back to shooting baskets.

Intently: Concentrating hard...it's showdown time.

arco explored for a while longer. Up this street, down that one. There was lots of shade, and the sidewalk felt cool under his feet. The streets were smooth and black. The asphalt hadn't given way to potholes. Everybody, it seemed, had their own driveway. "Yeah, it might be kinda cool living here," Marco thought.

Still, he had to admit he was starting to feel uncomfortable in this land of shuttered houses and close-cropped, crew-cut lawns. It was a little like the feeling he got whenever he walked into the school library. Suddenly, he felt a need to break the silence—to let everyone know he had arrived. "*HEY, WHERE IS EVERYONE?*" he shouted out. Then he broke into a run. When he reached the corner, he looked over his shoulder, half expecting someone to charge out of one of the big, shuttered houses and *SHUSH* him.

"HEY, WHERE IS EVERY-ONE?" he shouted out. Then he broke into a run.

On his block, kids chased each other around parked cars and played street ball. Girls jumped rope and played hopscotch on the sidewalk, while guys hustled passersby on the corner. Men and women sat on their stoops in the afternoon heat, fanning themselves and gossiping with their neighbors. Sometimes, on hot summer days, one of the neighborhood men would open a fire hydrant, and kids would come from blocks around to jump and dance in the spouting water. Marco listened for the sounds of laughter here. Except for the chatter of songbirds and the whir of a lawn-mower engine in the distance, he heard nothing.

Marco decided it was time to go **home**. He wanted to **play** some **baseball** with his **friends**.

When he got off the train at his station, he noticed only a few suits across the tracks, scurrying off to their cars in the parking lot. Rounding the corner of Glenwood Avenue, Marco saw a dandelion in bloom, poking its head out of a crack in the sidewalk. He reached down, picked it and stuffed it in his pocket as a present for his mother, in case she was angry about his being away all day. Looking up, he noticed police

cars with lights flashing and people milling around, grim-faced.

As Marco moved closer, he saw a boy lying still in the middle of the street, a dark red puddle gathering near his head, where his baseball cap had fallen. A medic was covering the boy with a yellow plastic sheet.

"Anthony was just 12," a woman was telling a TV reporter. "I saw two guys running down that alley..." someone else was saying to the officer in charge.

"AW,

man. That's the kid who hit the home run last night," Marco said to no one in particular, remembering the strength in the boy's long strides as he rounded the bases the night before.

Anguished: Feeling a sadness so big that it hurts inside.

Anthony had just moved to the neighborhood. Marco didn't know him well.

From the porch of Anthony's house came the sounds of *anguished* weeping. Marco took one more quick glance at the body laid out on the asphalt, *shrouded* by the plastic sheet. His stomach felt like it did the time he rode the big roller coaster with his friends at the amusement park last summer. He saw himself in the front car, *lurching* at the edge of a hundred-foot drop, looking down—straight down—at the tracks falling away from him atop webs of matchstick *trestle.* Marco wasn't screaming and howling the way he had then, but he was afraid he would start any minute if he didn't leave. "I've got to get away from here," he said and swung around abruptly to run to the practice field, thinking he'd skip supper and hang out until his friends arrived, hoping his mother would understand.

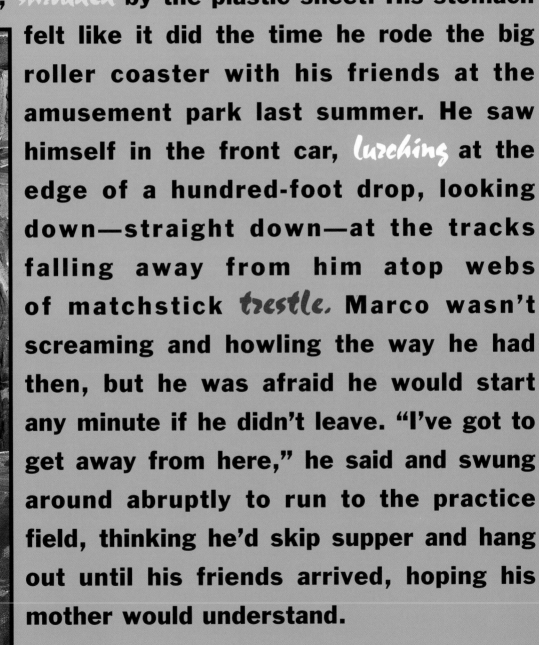

Shrouded: Covered by cloth...or, perhaps, in mystery.
Lurch: To stagger and sway, like a wino trying to make it to a park bench.
Trestle: A metal or wooden frame that lifts roller-coaster tracks to great heights.

Just then his mother hurried up to him from out of the crowd. The expression on her face told Marco that his baseball game was going to be called on account of blood. "You're not going anywhere tonight," she said in an angry, determined voice. Marco could feel her strong hand on his shoulder guiding him away from the **commotion** to the safety of their house. He was glad she was there.

Commotion: Lots of noise...people running around...you're not sure what's going to happen next.

Later that night, as he lay on the sofa watching the Reds pound the Phils, trying to forget the image of the plastic sheet on

Sleepily, Marco wondered whether games in those places were ever called on account of blood.

the pavement, he heard a whistle blow and felt the house rattle. The 10:40 train rumbled by. Sleepily, he thought about quiet places with tree-lined streets

and cool, shady sidewalks. Marco wondered whether games in those places were ever called on account of blood. "Ball four...he walks..." the TV announcer droned.

His mother came into the room then, carrying an old quilt his grandmother had made. Gently she covered him and whispered, "Don't forget, tomorrow is a busy day. We've got to..."

Marco didn't hear the rest. He was already asleep, dreaming of wicked curves and tracks that stretched halfway around the world. A train roared through his dream and came to a screeching halt in front of a crowded platform. There were corp'RATs everywhere. Mr. Shackleford was the conductor and his mother the engineer. Marco was there, too, wearing a blue pinstriped suit and his baseball cap. "How far can I go?" he asked the conductor. Then he climbed aboard.

His mother bent over and kissed her son good night. "Sweet dreams, Marco," she said in a low, soft voice. Marco rolled over, and as he did, a crumpled dandelion fell out of his pocket and landed on the floor.

a

reverse angle

production